For Daniel and Charlotte and the families
that fill their lives with love – M.O.

For Ava, and the More People who love her – A.G.

First published 2016 by Macmillan Children's Books
an imprint of Pan Macmillan
20 New Wharf Road, London N1 9RR
Associated companies throughout the world
www.panmacmillan.com

ISBN: 978-1-4472-7764-4 (HB)
ISBN: 978-1-5098-2129-7 (PB)

Text copyright © Mo O'Hara 2016
Illustrations copyright © Ada Grey 2016

Mo O'Hara and Ada Grey have asserted their rights to be identified as
the author and illustrator of this work in accordance with
the Copyright, Designs and Patents Act 1988.

1 3 5 7 9 8 6 4 2

A CIP catalogue record for this book is available from the British Library.

Printed in China

More People to Love Me

MO O'HARA   ADA GREY

MACMILLAN CHILDREN'S BOOKS

My family is huge!

Not tall kind of huge, more lots of people kind of huge.
But my step-brother Michael is super tall kind of huge too.

The only way I could really show how huge my family is would be to draw them.

And that's just what I had to do today in class.
Draw a family tree.

First I drew my daddy
and my sister Cee Cee.

Then I added my step-mum Sharon and my step-brother Michael. They live with my daddy.

Michael is a basketball player, so he needed lots of room for his long legs.

Next I drew my mummy, my step-dad David and their twins.

The twins didn't take up much room because they're not very big yet – but they can sure make a big noise when they want to.

Our teacher, Miss Sarah, said we could put in our pets as well. So I drew my tortoise, Happy.

But Happy didn't look very happy in my drawing because he doesn't like crowds or heights.

I had just about squashed everyone onto the page when
Miss Sarah said we had to put our grandparents in too.

I have a lot of grandparents! I didn't
know how I was going to make them all fit.

I started with Grandad and Granny
who are Daddy's mum and dad.

Then I added Grandpa Mark and Nana
who are Mummy's mum and her husband.

I also had to add Grandma Flo and
Pop-Pop who are Sharon's mum and dad,

and Grandpa and Helen who
are Mummy's dad and his wife.

And I couldn't forget Grananna. She's David's mum, Anna.
We got to make up any grand-name for her as long as it
didn't make her sound too old!

I tried really, really hard to fit everybody into my family tree.

I squashed and I squeezed.

But there are so many people,
they just wouldn't fit.

I didn't want any of them to think I didn't
love them because they weren't on my tree.

A tear rolled down my cheek and onto the paper.
It smudged my mummy and one of the babies too.

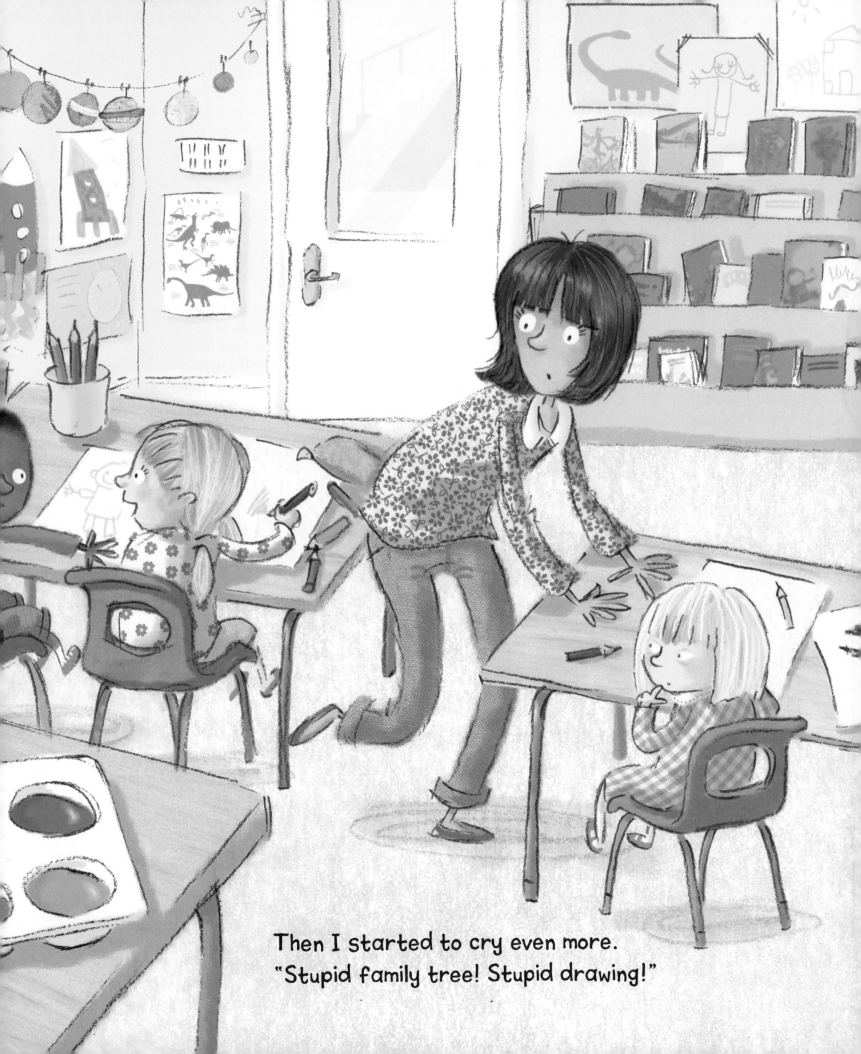

Then I started to cry even more.
"Stupid family tree! Stupid drawing!"

Miss Sarah wiped my eyes and blotted the tear off the page.

The baby was still a little smudged, but Miss Sarah said, "Babies are messy so they usually look a little smudged anyway."

Then I told her about not everybody fitting in my tree.
"You have a lot of special people in your life!" said Miss Sarah.
"I know," I nodded, "and I don't want to leave anyone out."

"With all those special people, I think you need an extra
special tree," said Miss Sarah. "I have an idea!"

We drew and coloured and taped bits together until everybody fitted in.

There was just one person missing . . .

"Don't forget to add yourself," said Miss Sarah.

When we all got up to tell the class about our family trees, it took me a while.

After I'd had my turn, my friend Sally asked,
"Is it hard having a huge family like that?"

I smiled and said, "Nah, there are just more people
to love me! And who needs a family tree anyway . . .

"when you can have a family forest?"